A

Deafening

Absence

Stories by

CHRIS S. WITWER

Published by Felsputzer Press.

ISBN: 979-8-218-97097-0

Copyright © 2024 by Felsputzer Press. First edition.

Cover and back cover art copyright @2024 by April Laragy Stein. https://artisanworks.net/artist/april-laragy-stein/

Published in the United States of America. All rights reserved.

This book is lovingly dedicated to my wife,
my love, my ardent champion, Shi.

* * *

Many thanks to April Laragy Stein, Bryan Ochalla,
David Schowengerdt, and Jennifer Morris. This would
be a different book without you. My gratitude also to
Linda Zietlow for her enduring support and kindness.

Certain oddities in punctuation, use of or lack of use quotations around dialogue, and special formatting in some stories are on purpose to create a certain feel, sound, and pacing of the words. Any typos, however, are entirely the fault of gremlins.

"Stories are for joining the past to the future. Stories are for those late hours in the night when you can't remember how you got from where you were to where you are. Stories are for eternity, when memory is erased, when there is nothing to remember except the story."

- Tim O'Brien,
The Things They Carried

Contents

Not Today

H E PULLED IN slowly to avoid startling her where she knelt pruning the prissy pink rosebush. Seeing him, she removed her gardening gloves one finger at a time, smiled and waved.

I brought peaches, he said as he settled the paper sack into the crook of his arm.

Oh, you went to Fredericksburg. I didn't know. How lovely.

He mounted the three metal steps into the pristine trailer, lined up his boots on the mat, set the fruit on the counter. Not a crumb to be seen, not a thing out of place. The hand towel under the sink was folded in thirds, perfectly centered on the little bar she hung it on. Later, she would suggest they eat the juicy peaches outdoors under the dampening sky. No mess.

She's worked hard to keep this place up. To pay it off, to repair the big things when they needed repairing. To manipulate the tiny yard and corner garden to her will. He mustn't complain. He was lucky to be allowed inside at all these past two years.

He dropped into the lazy chair, cracked a beer, turned on the game. Through the window he watched her stand, clap the dirt off the knees of her gardening pants, reach for the hose. A tiny squeak, then the splat of a small stream as she toured the four corners, giving everything a cool drink. He caught a whiff of the tomato vines, the cilantro, mint and peppers and basil. And finally, the damp earth that almost but didn't quite smell like worms. In a moment she'd come in to change. She'd pour a glass of iced tea, finish the daily crossword, start dinner.

Routine soothed them both. They'd become accustomed to one another, themselves, their histories.

He, divorced. She, married. He, lonely. She, waiting. Hoping. Knowing what her future held. He, not so much. He only knew there would be an end, and that he'd have no control over when he would have to start his life all over again. She would dictate that. Or, more accurately, the State of Texas would dictate that.

For now, beer and football games, gardening and sun tea, and delicious dinners of warmed smokehouse brisket, fresh sliced tomatoes, rolls rising in the oven.

At night under the crisp white sheets, he'd forget there was a limit. He'd place his roughened hands on her soft wide hips, pull her onto himself, smile as she mounted him. Feel her lips on his mostly bare dome, feel her small breasts lightly brushing his chest from above. Then eyes closed, he would pretend. Pretend she really meant it and wasn't thinking of her husband, the one who would one day return and ruin what comfort he found here.

He closed his ears in case she got his name wrong.

She never did. She couldn't. He was no match at all, just a placeholder.

One day the phone would ring, collect from jail, would he accept? That collect call would be her dream come true. She wouldn't say when she expected the call, wouldn't speak of it or of Him at all. But he knew even though he pretended not to. The phone, it scared him. The mailman too. He didn't know which messenger to fear most, but that fear sat in his gut. Hot and acidic, fermenting.

One day, but not today. Today there would be juicy Fredericksburg peaches and cool grass under bare feet, lightning bugs appearing and disappearing in the night breezes.

Jingle Ass

EVERYBODY STEALS. ESPECIALLY my sister, who steals from me and our neighbors and who knows who all else, then comes here and does it while sneering right into the security camera during my shifts. Makeup, usually. Or clothes. After she's gone, I erase the tapes. I'm not letting her ruin this for me. This is my first job that doesn't involve pretzels or lawnmowers.

From my perch behind the controls, I see Boss emerge through the double doors onto the sales floor. His loose apple shape sways with every step as he aims his soft old body toward the attempted, thwarted crime. He isn't in a hurry. You can tell he used to be a cop.

Walking past the commotion, Boss turns a corner, stops out of sight where he can listen a minute. He's figuring out what's going on, how dangerous it is. Doesn't want to have to explain to Corporate why two of his staff are in the hospital with road rash again. (That was such a rush!) Or how all those parked cars got smashed on his watch. (I love this job!)

Boss reaches for his walkie, whispers to me, "Watch Jingle Ass, the big one with all the keys on her belt. I want a good record."

Which means he thinks he's going to have to file a police report, or maybe even arrest her. This is where I really shine. I'm not the strongest or the fastest, but I do have a knack for knowing which camera to use next so I don't ever lose sight of the important thing – a right hand, a back pocket, a face. My coworkers think I'm good at camera tracking because my generation plays a lot of video games. But truth is, I never have. Arcades are boring. Unlike this job.

Two women at the return desk have an open box that looks like maybe a circular saw. It's hard to tell. I don't see a receipt. Jingle Ass is pretty angry, might've been red-faced if the camera were in color but it isn't. Her small companion is staring at the floor, silent. She looks cowed. Resigned to whatever is going to happen next.

Jingle Ass has a comb in her back pocket, a thick men's wallet, no purse. She's got a wide rat's tail. Isn't wearing a bra but totally should be.

She turns toward Boss as he approaches. He knows where the dome camera is, so I have a great angle.

Man oh man is she pitching a fit. On the monitors I see heads turning throughout the store, clear across Sporting Goods all the way to Children's. One lady grabs her toddler and leaves. Someday we'll have audio to go with the tapes. What a game changer that'll be. For now, we write long reports and it's all "he said, she said" for the cops and lawyers.

Lighting a Marlboro, I put my feet up on the console. Watch them argue a while. Boss is not going to change his mind. Jingle Ass is getting madder and madder, talks with her hands, gets too close to his face. I can see his shoulder muscles tense up. He's ready. She's going down hard if she doesn't back off.

Just then, Bobby comes into view about to clock in. I grab the desk phone, push pound six and make an overhead announcement, "L5 to Customer Service. L5 to Customer Service please" so nice and friendly. L5 is our code for 'come give somebody some backup.' Bobby knows I'm talking to him because there's nobody else here yet. He does the same thing Boss did – gets close, stays out of sight, listens. Good. If Boss has to tackle Jingle Ass, Bobby can help.

Like that time he put some asshole in a headlock for me. I never would've done that. Also, I am not fast enough but Bobby is. He put that man's head in the crook of his arm, tightening like a vise. I could see every one of Bobby's body-builder bicep muscles bulging, Von Erich style, and then right down the inside of his curl Bobby's skin split apart, opening a long thin line that dripped a clear runny liquid.

Steroids.

But we got the guy, and we sent him to jail, so there's that.

Jingle Ass finally backs down. She's still pissed, still arguing, but has decided not to end up with her arms pinned behind her back, face down on the cold tile, handcuffs biting into her thick wrists. She yells and kicks the door on the way out, knocking her mousy sidekick over.

Boss looks up at the camera. He does that when the show is over. I'm not sure why. I know the show is over.

He starts to shuffle back toward the office, squeezes the walkie, "Call the Dallas store and give them a heads up. She'll try again."

10-4.

Then he says, "Fucking dyke."

And my whole body responds with a sickening wave; gut to heart to head. I forget to breathe. Cheeks burn, fever hot.

Fucking Boss.

Janey Got A Gun

C'MON, LET'S WALK, she said. You're not doing shit.

I groaned, got up, put my cigarette out. We're locked in, I said. Where can we go?

She laughed. They didn't tell you? We can go to the athletic track from 10 to 1 just don't miss lunch.   Bring your little radio.

Janey was short, and sweet. She spoke with a Texican accent, faster when excited or angry. I liked her. It was hard to imagine knowing her outside this environment. She lived somewhere dangerous that gave her rough edges. But I liked her.

Those short legs moved as fast as her tongue. I huffed and puffed to keep up.

Listen, she said. People come here once and never come back. Or they come here over and over and over.

How about you? I asked, challenged to breathe while moving so fast. Depression makes you lazy and I had been lazy a long time.

Third time, she said. There will be at least five. Then I'll either be stuck in a place like this forever, or I'll be dead. Muerte. I can't really tell yet. But I will never be free.

I didn't know what to say. I said something lame about third time's a charm and not counting herself out quite yet. She ignored me.

You, she said, you have a chance. I figured it out. Some people, they come here once and that's it. But if you come back even once, it'll never end. Don't come back. Do whatever it takes to keep from coming back. Get your shit together and don't come back. Okay?

I nodded, unsure. Without warning, the Twelve Steps mantra, "Keep coming back," played in my head.

O-Kay? she asked again.

Okay, I said, still unsure.

I wondered why she kept coming back. What might make us different.

Think about who's here, she said. What their stories are. You can see it too, if you try. Think of someone, anyone.

The old man, I said.

Damn, hard one first. Okay. The old man. Harry, I think. Yeah, he's been somewhere over and over. They don't do shock therapy until you have no other choice.

He makes me sad. Just looking at him when he's done. Each week he is less himself, more confused.

Janey added, Have you seen his wife? Heartbreaking. She comes in here and just, damn. Her life with him is over. He's a child now.

Is that permanent? I asked, hoping not.

I don't know. Think of someone else.

Marjorie.

Yes, Marjorie. She was here last year at least twice. She runs away a lot. Did they put you in the same room?

Yeah.

They're hoping you'll tell them when she runs away again.

No shit?

Yeah. Do the right thing. Don't cover for her, it's a pattern.

Like Brock?

OMG yeah, like Brock. Janey laughed. Whose lighter did he palm to start that fire?

I just raised my hand, lowered my head in shame.

Well now you're not so naïve are you? she laughed.

The bedsheet incident though, that killed me. Him trying to hang himself with bedsheets.

We didn't say much for a while.

He's so young, I finally said. How can he be so hurt, so depressed?

Janey didn't know either. But she said he'd probably end up with shock therapy himself someday if they couldn't figure out some way to help him.

I noticed that she didn't put the onus on Brock. Not like she did with me. Did she think I was more able? Less damaged? I was afraid to ask, so I didn't.

The Dallas rock station was playing the latest hits. Harder rock than I usually listened to. The next song seemed to start with groaning or humming. We had MTV at home, so even I knew it was Steven Tyler.

Oh, that's my song! Turn it up!

I did, and we walked faster. I didn't know the words yet, but Janey sure did.

She sang along with the band about her daddy, her gun, how she's never going to be the "saaa,aaaa,aaaame!"

Fuck. This is her song??

She was energized. Buoyed somehow. We stopped to play air guitar.

Careful, she warned, nodding toward the nurse sitting on a bench, making notes on a clipboard. They'll think we've cracked up even more. And you don't want those kind of drugs, trust me.

Did you got a gun, Janey? I asked, trying to be clever.

Don't ask questions you don't want the answer to, she said brusquely.

How old are you? I asked.

Older than you think. And I got an old soul, too.

Me, too! I'm Pisces!

She scoffed. Not the same, chica. Not the same.

We walked a while more, huffing. I felt my heart pounding as I really started to sweat. I could barely catch my breath, and I could smell blood in my nose. And dust, Texas dirt.

I should quit smoking, learn to run.

Look, there's Emily, Janey said. She is WHACK. Stay away from her.

What do you mean? She's nice. She gave me her cookie at dinner last night.

That's how it starts. Just, … look. When do you get out?

Thursday.

Well then. Don't come back. I never want to see you again.

Lemon Pledge Shirt

I'M GLAD YOU like your new shirt so much. I didn't realize it would be so comfortable. It just reminded me of, do you remember when women started wearing their husbands' old shirts, untucked, sleeves rolled 2/3 up, with rollers in their hair? This was right after they realized they didn't have to get all made up to leave - or clean - the house. Early 70s.

I can't tell you your new shirt reminds me of my mom. You'd just rip it off and take it out on the patio and burn it in effigy. But it makes me think of her that one year - just the one, where she was a little rebellious in a totally socially acceptable way. It may have been the year she smoked cigarettes. There was one year she was... different. In between my sisters being born. Might've been the year of the super tornado outbreak. My memory smells of Lemon Pledge.

We had this long stereo console, dark wood and long with a top that raised up. You could polish it til you saw your reflection in the heavy wood. There was red velvet lining inside. And man, that thing was a bitch to dust. There were these intricate wood curlicues on the front, across the speaker fabric, that collected dust so bad.

Anyway I associate your new shirt for some reason with the smell of Lemon Pledge, open windows and curtains dancing in the spring breezes, while we sang along to - I kid you not - "I'd Like to Teach the World to Sing (In Perfect Harmony)."

Must've been the year I was five.

Lazy Afternoon

W E WERE LYING on our stomachs in the grass, lazily searching through the clover for luck. The day was sunny and slightly warm. A light breeze cooled our skin.

"What's the first thing you remember?" he asked.

"Ever?" I answered.

"Yeah."

"Let me think." I rolled onto my back, shifting a little to avoid the press of root sticking through the dirt.

"Ever?"

"Yeah."

I thought for a while, watching the weeping willow sway above us.

"Probably the smell of my baby sister's puke. Or her constant screaming until she puked."

He laughed. "Tell me something better."

"You first," I said.

He didn't think long. "Okay. Baby ducks. I remember walking in the grass near the pond, over there, and there was a row of baby duckies toddling about, playing follow the leader. My babysitter didn't let me chase them."

"Who were you with? How old were you?"

"No idea. Young."

"That's a sweet memory," I said. "Let me try again."

Puffy white clouds marched overhead, dissipating or morphing with surprising efficiency.

"I remember the tornadoes of course. You do too."

"Yep," he said. "But that can't be a first memory. Definitely a childhood memory, but not first. Try again."

"Well, let's give credit though. The tornado, that is for sure the strongest memory I have, even now. It's like, a groove scarred into my brain," I said.

"Your body, too," he added before tapping my wrist with his finger.

I caught a whiff of tangy alfalfa in the air. Then, "How about the Mexican jumping bean affair? When my cousin and I left them where the younger kids could eat them?"

He just laughed.

This was harder than I would have expected. "Um, the smell of Folgers coffee before dad poured it into his thermos and left for work?"

"Closer…"

"I know! Grandma's record player! '(How Much Is) That Doggie in the Window?' The plastic record was orange and we played it all the time!"

"Yes!" He smiled.

"I never understood why a doggie would be in a window. Seriously, made no sense," I said.

"That's funny," he said. "I guess you hadn't seen a pet store yet."

"On that same note," I added, "'Puff, the Magic Dragon' made perfect sense. Even before I started smoking pot."

I told him a lot of my memories involved music. Lyrics, storytelling. He wasn't surprised.

I began to hum then. "What's a skippy do dad day?"

"Oh! Oh! The happiest girl song?" he asked.

"Yes! That one. 'The Happiest Girl in the Whole U.S.A.'" I sang it loud.

He waited for the little tear to fall from my eye, down my cheek to where I could flick it off.

We sat with the silence a while. He picked a false lucky clover.

"You know what's really sad?" I asked.

"What?"

"I think you should be able to roller skate with buffaloes," I said proudly.

He sprang up, planted his feet, locked his fists on his hips, "Doesn't matter, you can still be happy!"

"That's not how it goes!!" We both laughed. What a silly song.

We righted our bikes and rode off, side by side like some kind of comedy skit.

"What's the one about a watermelon patch?" he asked.

"OMG I can't believe you even remembered that!"

We laughed and pedaled and chased each other, cycling zigzags on the blacktop.

My Nephew Fishing

M Y NEPHEW SAYS he's just been fishing. He's taken photos to prove it, leaving small fish on the ground near the pond's edge, and using his smart phone to photograph the fish alongside his size 11 shoe for size comparison. But I do not believe him.

He was not here last night. His truck just rambled back up the gravel road at 5 am this morning, and he posted the photos a few minutes later... from inside his trailer. Where has he been, and why is he trying to convince people he's been fishing when it doesn't look like he has been? I'm tempted to ask, so I tighten my robe and put out my smoke. I refill my coffee cup and head to his door.

There in the driveway is his truck, covered in mud and muck. I'm almost relieved, until I see the sheriff's car coming down the path to our family compound, as it's sometimes called. A compound of trailers, right. It's at this point that I smell the gun oil, or whatever he uses to clean the guns he totes around with him everywhere he goes now that he lives out here.

This is the moment I have to decide whether to go fishing myself, or to choose ignorance. My stomach churns as I await the sheriff's own fishing expedition.

A Deafening Absence

CARL BRENNER IS a lifeguard instructor with COPD. It's so hard to breathe sometimes he can barely hold his breath anymore at all. And his body is no longer lithe and swift underwater.

Even so, Carl is still a very good lifeguard instructor. He is still a lifesaver.

Carl's students – his kids - are the best lifeguards in the entire Finger Lakes region. They are strong, sure, always on alert - capable of laser-like focus, and they save lives because of it.

If you ever hear a young person bark "no running" at the mall or at the grocer's, it's probably one of Carl's kids engaging in reflexive correction. Reflexive protection. Reflexive guarding of life.

People say, "if a swimmer can be saved, Carl's kids will save that swimmer."

Carl lives near the water, of course, where he feels most at home. He hears the lively river from his kitchen where he has just made himself a simple dinner.

He takes his meal to the porch to watch the sun melt into a pastel sky. They call this the golden hour. Carl loves the magic of it. Buzzing mosquitoes chased by hungry bats, cicadas getting louder and louder, an unseen owl hoots in the distance, beginning his evening hunt. Lightning bugs softly click tick clicking - flashing beacons in motion. This is Carl's own private sundown serenade.

Though tonight's serenade is punctuated by a new sound, something syncopated, irregular. Something intermittent. What is it?

He sets down his whiskey glass.

Could it be a fishing boat? A party? No, not out here. A kayaker? Unlikely. The water is too swift, the day too late.

Carl listens with his whole body.

Ice cubes shift and clink.

Then he hears it again, and his heart races. Someone is afraid. Someone might be in danger.

He waits.

There it is again. Clear, distinct, a human cry carried above the river, moving his direction.

If a swimmer can be saved, Carl's kids will save that swimmer.

Can Carl save a swimmer still?

He runs to the bank, cursing his flat feet and gorilla arms – no good on land.

When he first spots her, she is just a head bobbing up and down like a hairy coconut. Then her arms pierce the water, reaching in panic.

He kicks off his boots, slogs into the river.

Cold, but not dangerous. Not yet. Not like the last time he tried to pull a drowning girl out of dark water at dusk.

Who gets a second chance at that?

Carl powers his way toward her now. He thinks he'll be able to grab her as long as she stays afloat.

He fills his burning lungs as best he can and strokes toward her. Hopes he doesn't have to dive under to try to find her.

But he knows how cruel nature can be.

He was just fourteen back then. A good swimmer already. He could have been a dolphin. He was made to get wet, take in huge gulps of air, and glide gracefully or shoot cleanly through it. Underwater, he felt utterly beautiful. Weightless, clean, caressed by the liquid cool.

But sad, always sad too. A sad, lonely dolphin.

Miracle of miracles, he intercepts the coconut-headed young woman. She seems to faint just as he catches hold of her, her head dropping into the water. In lifeguarding sessions, Carl teaches how to help an unresponsive victim – and he does it now. He leans her back against his chest, catches her arm with his, presses his palm to her forehead to keep her mouth above the water.

They are being flung downstream together. Soon though, Carl sees red lights flashing in the distance. Rescuers are racing to a bridge downstream, hoping to pluck her free.

What a relief. He isn't alone with her. He needs help. So far Carl has completely failed to steer their bodies ashore. The water is too fast and too strong. But they'll be nearer the riverbank down by the bridge where surely a human chain will pull them out. If that doesn't work, there is a wide curve after the bridge that should slow the river, giving him another shot at saving them both.

The water tastes green and muddy. He spits. He wheezes. His chest hurts.

No more cigars, Carl.

He wonders if any of his kids are there to help. He hopes so. He is tiring and his chest grows tighter in the cold.

Just then Carl is punched in the face by the unfairness. That he is now rescuing an absolute stranger but never had the chance to do the same for his baby sister.

Ellie was four, with thick black hair. Black like the depths that would quietly, savagely claim her.

Nobody heard her fall in. Later the police called it preposterous that a four-year-old child, essentially a 40-pound toddler, could fall overboard without anyone seeing or hearing it. But that's exactly what happened. There were four boys and 2 grown men on the skiff that day. The winds were calm, waters were still, the flat-bottomed boat unmoving as the late afternoon sky faded away. No music, no rambunctious laughter. Nothing.

Still, she was gone before anyone noticed.

Carl was the one who felt her absence first. Why had it taken so long?

He stood, scanned the boat left right left, his stomach lurching. She wasn't there. "ELLIE!!?" he screamed.

Carl tried to peer around each of his brothers, hoping she'd made herself small enough to hide behind one of them.

"Ellie!" he called out as he spun Rory's shoulders, to look behind him. Not there.

"Ellie!" he shoved Bobby.

"Ellie!" Kevin's turn.

Someone asked if we left her at the dock?

No! Ellie!

Carl dove off the back of the boat, sneakers and all. Everyone else began calling her name with increasing panic. Ellie! Like they could find her just by screaming her name louder and louder in increasingly high registers. Ellie!

Young Carl's head surfaced, teeth chattering, "Pull in your fucking lines!" he yelled as his brothers began following him into the water. Even through the fog of shock, dad held little Rory back. He was only seven.

They never found her, not ever. At times it almost felt like she had never existed at all. At others, her absence was the loudest thing in the world. Even now as the swirling river slapped his ears, Carl heard Ellie's absence.

The young woman in his arms stirs. She is alive.

The bridge is close. A spotlight illuminates the fire truck. Carl hears a disembodied voice over a loudspeaker.

"Aim for the net!"

Carl can't see a net, nothing but water and fading sky, the low wooden bridge, and the big red truck next to it.

"Grab the net!"

Carl propels himself up as much as he can. Searchlights cross in front of him. Before he has time to hope, he is tangled in a net. With her. She is gulping, crying.

"Hold on! We're pulling you out. Hold on!"

Carl does. He holds on. As they pull him and the girl toward shore, men in yellow coats and shiny black boots swarm the bank, arms outstretched. "I'm sorry," she cries. "I didn't mean it." They get her, pull her up away from him, toward the steep mossy bank.

Carl suddenly feels too cold. He isn't holding the net anymore. But rescuers are here to help. He isn't alone.

Then suddenly, he is.

Alone.

Cold.

In the dark, a little disoriented in the roaring river.

He wonders what Ellie felt that day. Was she confused? Was she scared too?

He hears the firemen hollering after him. Probably something important, but he can't hear what.

The river does not slow after the bridge. It gets faster, darker, colder. Menacing. Carl is in the biting current, hurtling toward wherever the water is taking him. He is not in control.

The dolphin within is gone.

And Ellie's absence is, once again, deafening.

No Priest

H E SAT FACING the window, mindlessly watching the barren fields and drab towns pass by as the train swayed and lurched. The seats were green and wide, pleather like on the ferries he used to take to the island.

Today he was alone in a car full of commuters, headed to the capital to conduct whatever business they had. He was going to court and both his stomach and his fast-beating heart knew it.

Ryan went over his testimony in his head. Starting and stopping, starting and stopping – would he be able to get through it in front of the judge and the lawyers, and... *him*? He surely hoped so. He started over, this time running through it quickly not changing the sentences as he thought them but racing through the script like you'd race through the end of a good book just to see how it ended. Racing past the word he'd...

"Excuse me, is this seat taken?" asked a tall slim man with a friendly face and a white collar contrasted against his otherwise black attire. A priest, no doubt.

Ryan nodded at the empty bench seat facing his, to indicate the priest was welcome to take it. He offered a weak. distracted smile before going back to mentally rehearsing what he would say later today in the city, in the courtroom, in front of the lawyers and the jury and the monster.

The priest sat. "Thank you, thank you very much."

That should've been the end of it.

Ryan was conscious that his lips wanted to move as he practiced his phrases. The most vivid, the ones describing the mud and blood and gore, the ones he couldn't ever forget but that today he had to practice anyway lest he avoid them when they counted the most. When they belonged not just in his head or in his nightmares, but in a large room filled with educated men listening. Listening. Listening, to him.

"I'm headed to Ottawa. You?" The priest opened a newspaper, smiled at Ryan over the top of it.

Ryan nodded again. The priest raised the paper and began to read in silence until a few miles later, he asked, "Would you watch my things?" as he rose.

"Of course."

The priest walked slowly toward the back of the car, steadying himself by lightly grabbing the back of each aisle he passed. Like you would on a plane, when your feet don't really believe they're on the ground.

Ryan glanced at the priest's satchel. A nice one, black and shiny, well-kept. It was plump with what Ryan imagined were scholarly texts. Priests, they study a lot, right? Study the word of god and of the men who say they know the word of god, and of the men who describe other men who say they know the word of their imaginary god.

He felt petty. He looked out the window again. They were passing some brick row houses backed up against the tracks, laundry hanging on the rails, dirt yards no grass. Poverty looks the same here as it does at home.

Ryan noticed his feet were cold. Almost numb, as if he'd walked a long way in a cold rain. Which he had not. The day was clear and chilly, and there was only a dusting of snow on the ground.

The priest returned with two paper cups of coffee. "I took the opportunity to grab a coffee and couldn't see myself not offering you one as well. How do you take it?" the friendly priest asked.

Funny. Priests drink coffee? I guess so, they aren't nuns, he thought. Then again, he remembered where the name cappuccino supposedly came from - the capuchin monks, who wore brown robes with white hoods on top. But maybe they didn't actually drink the coffee? Ryan didn't know.

He thanked the priest, gratefully took the warm cup, declined the one with milk that the priest seemed to hope would be his.

The warm liquid soothed Ryan's dry throat. Ryan felt obliged to return the kindness with conversation. "Beautiful day, isn't it?"

"It is yes. I shall rejoice and be glad in it." Then he asked, "Do you believe in God young man?"

Well. So that was fast. No way to direct the conversation away from the elephant in the train car now.

"I do not. Never have."

The priest frowned slightly, then smiled directly into Ryan's eyes.

Oh great, Ryan thought. He thinks this is an opportunity. It is not.

But the priest didn't say anything for a few minutes. Then, gently, "That's ok. God says you're on the right path."

Startled, Ryan responded, "The god you believe in says it's ok I don't believe in god, any god? What if I'm an atheist?"

The priest simply nodded over his cup o' joe. Ryan thought, if there actually is a god, it's in that cup. The caffeinated elixir, the balm of Gilead. Yes, coffee reigns supreme. There is no higher power. He was giddy now.

Suddenly, Ryan felt the urge to cry. He supposed it was the priest's kindness, and possibly his faith. Ryan had often envied those who believed. The people who could fool themselves into a comforting, loving relationship with their imaginary friend, Santa in the sky.

But this was different. The priest had something special, something healing.

Ryan squirmed in his seat. He felt the need to practice his testimony again as the train grew closer to his destination. He gulped down the rest of the coffee, thanked the priest, turned to the window.

The priest simply waited.

Not long after, the train made a stop and a few people disembarked. The car had more air in it now. There were open seats if he needed one. But what he really needed was to pee.

The priest was reading a book of affirmations and smiling to himself as he read. Perhaps the priest was a little touched in the head.

"Would you watch my things while I go to the restroom?" Ryan touched his book bag, to indicate what needed watching.

"Of course. Take your time."

Ryan opened the accordioned metal door between cars, found the water closet, then sought out more coffee. One for him, one for the priest. Milk for them both this time.

But when he returned to their car, the seats were empty.

Ryan did a double-take. Checked the row number. Car number. Noticed the same people sitting where he'd left them.

He looked under the foot rack, and above, in the hat rack, for his bag. His notebook. But there was nothing. They were gone.

Ryan searched his mind for a plausible explanation. Perhaps the priest also had to answer nature's call and had taken Ryan's things with him for safekeeping. Optimism and hope took over.

Ryan sat and sipped.

He shifted his buttocks, as he often did to make sure he could feel his wallet in his back pocket.

This time, it was gone.

What. The. Hell.

He'd never get inside the courtroom without an ID. They'd been very clear about that in the letter they sent him. Plus he needed his notes, the maps, the bus fare. What. The. Hell.

He tried to slow his beating heart, to tell himself there must be a reasonable explanation. They would laugh about it later.

The minutes ticked away.

And ticked.

And continued ticking until a sick, sour feeling rose from Ryan's belly. He began a search. Car to car to car. No priest.

He went back the other direction, slowly, looking everyone in the eye as he passed, hoping for recognition. Car to car to car. No priest.

The conductor hadn't seen him, no. "Was there a priest on this train? I never saw one," he added. Then, "where's your ticket young man?" Fortunately, the stub was still in his shirt pocket.

But now Ryan began to truly panic. He had to testify. It was the only way to end the years-long torment. To lock that bastard up for good. To get his life back.

To get his life back.

Ryan talked to everyone in a uniform, even the cashier in the café car. He walked the entire length of the train over and over, not knowing what else to do. He began to sweat. His breath was loud and wet. Other passengers began to notice him with worry lines slicing across their foreheads. Fuck. Fuck. Fuck.

He stopped in the wheelchair area, which was empty but had a bigger window where he could look outside as the train bolted down the track. Trees. Dirt. Another small town coming up, one that smelled like it had a papermill.

If Ryan believed in God, this would be the time to beg.

Damn it.

The train slowed, then stopped. Nobody near Ryan moved toward the door as it opened, so he did. He stepped onto the lowest metal step and leaned out. He didn't know if he could get back on if he disembarked, so he just leaned out. Nobody got off any of the cars. Three ladies in big purple hats were getting on, like it was Sunday or something, even though it wasn't.

The "door closing" warning sounded. Ryan had no choice but to step back and let the doors shut. At least nobody got off the train here, so the priest was still aboard somewhere.

The train chuffed and slowly made its way past the platform. That's when Ryan saw him. The priest, without his collar, Ryan's bag tucked under his elbow. He was watching the train depart, looking through the windows as it pulled away. When he spotted Ryan, he grinned widely and waved as if to say, so long sucka!

Fuck! That man was no goddamned priest after all.

The train was already gaining speed, and even as Ryan pounded on the doors and called out STOP! and looked for the emergency brake, he knew it was useless. The not-priest had just set the monster free.

Three Men

THREE MEN SIT around a deck of cards placed on the pale earth, under a scorching sun. Parched, all. Their skin is thick, reddened like their eyes. Dark hair in greasy clumps grows down the back of their necks.

The older one deals, and the other two fan their cards out in their swollen, oil-stained hands. It's almost too hot to play. They better get this game over with so the young skinny one can slide up under the truck to nap in the shade.

The other two will make do elsewhere. And there they'll stay until dusk when the mosquitoes make it worthwhile to start a fire.

Red and Black Stripes

ROSIE IS A stocky, youngish Latina with short hair shaved on the sides. She wears aqua scrubs which really bring out the intricate tattoos up and down both her muscular forearms. She could probably carry a full keg in each hand if she wanted. You can tell that she doesn't put up with shit from anybody. And yet, she doesn't need to fight the inevitable all the time either.

Her station wafts light jazz across the linoleum. She once worked for a private company that drew blood in a business office, and they put the blood draw chair in a carpeted room. Dumb asses. It was not her place to warn them, but she did anyway, and as often happens when she sticks her nose where it doesn't belong, they made her clean the spilled blood twice before installing linoleum like they should have done.

Sometimes she needs to take a deep breath, letting people do what they're gonna do. Because they're gonna anyway.

Does jazz keep blood pressure down? Or music in general? Perhaps. Can't hurt, and nobody here at the hospital has complained yet. Somebody will complain someday, and then she'll get wireless earbuds and go about her business.

A man sits in her chair. She approaches him with a gentle energy, casually monitoring him for signs of distress but not making him aware of it. "Which arm?" she asks.

He crooks his left and taps it twice, quickly, with his right hand. "If I'm too dehydrated you can use the right too. Everybody seems to do that lately."

She raises an eyebrow slightly, thinking that everyone else needs to be more patient. Or just better.

She moves in, ever so slowly, uses her fingers to highlight the vein she wants and swabs it before inserting the needle. He doesn't even wince. One tube, two. Three, then four. One red and black stripes, two pinks, and a lavender.

He thinks of the last time he went to the strip bar. Red and black stripes, two pinks, and a lavender.

It's over before he knows it, no bleeding. It's not even going to bruise this time.

He wonders if he's seen her before, shakes his head. No way.

She tapes gauze over the puncture site, and as she touches him, he smells her cologne. A men's cologne not usually worn by straight women. Calvin Kline Obsession.

Red and black stripes.

He realizes she gave him a lap dance years ago, and drew blood with her teeth giving him a hickey in his chair. A very different kind of chair. He wishes he could see her tramp stamp now but then stops himself and decides never to think that way again. She's no tramp. She's a healer. He needed her then, just as he needs her now to make sure his meds are working.

Maybe she put herself through nursing school with that money. Maybe she just had a couple hard years or was raising kids alone. None of his business then, none of his business now.

Old Guy Manicure

O LD WHITE GUY at Asian Fusion.

Short, big paunch, mostly bald with a short ring of hair remaining in a curve around the back of his head.

Slumped, hands forward and nails out toward pert little Vietnamese woman with reading glasses atop her head. She's no nonsense. Big shiny earrings chomping gum.

He says, "You ladies sure make a lot of noise for being so small."

She doesn't respond. Chomp chomp. Smack.

He repeats it.

She gives a minimal, distracted grunt as if she's too busy to reply.

He looks up at me, nods, grins, wants me to agree it's funny. He wants to feel funny.

Then he sits there quietly until time for the forearm massage. He giggles, embarrassed.

Now she laughs readily, heartily.

Eviction

T HERE WAS A mad dash, five or six people in cars and pickups all parked along the snaking driveway, just far enough away you couldn't see from any of the residences. Youngish people, different races, two women from the leasing office, four men. Oh no, five.

There was an older confused looking old guy in slippers and a faded white undershirt just pacing slouched and aimless while everyone else moved furniture around quick-like. It was a bit of a fire drill, chaotic and confusing, musical dining chairs flying out of a truck bed. The whole thing took under three minutes.

Later, when everyone was all gone, you could see what was left on the sidewalk under the shade trees. A mattress, a box spring, a table four chairs a bureau. Shirts. An ironing board.

Had it been scavenged so quickly? Or was that it?

Social Letters

Dear Susan,

It has been longer than I meant it to be. I apologize for hurting your feelings.

You know that I'm a Christian, right? And that I don't always read everything I post on social media? I got that from a friend and didn't read it before posting.

But I do need you to know that I am a Christian and always will be.

I miss you,

- Bonnie

***

Bonnie,

It's good to hear from you, I've missed you too. Has it been a whole year since we emailed?

A quick update – I got hired full time and we're finally getting settled in here a little. Still working from home though, so will have plenty of local sites to explore in the future. Jay's health is still a challenge. We mask everywhere still, and avoid public places when we can.

I hope you and Mike and both your families are well, and that you have a warm and wonderful holiday season.

- Susan

***

Susan,

We are well, yes. Mike got vaccinated and had a terrible heart problem from it, so the doctor said no more vaccines. I am not vaccinated, and we both had COVID last fall but got better. Mike's daughter and family are also unvaccinated and have recovered. My son and daughter, and their spouses, and all the grandkids are also unvaccinated. When we all got COVID at the same time, the kids didn't even get it. They still played football and went to school.

The Lord saw fit to take our pastor to Heaven just before Christmas, so we've been at the church a lot lately helping out. He died doing what he loved – praying. We think it's pretty special he died while talking directly to the Lord. I wonder what they were talking about.

- Bonnie

* * *

Hi Bonnie,

I want to go back to something you said in your first email – you asked if I knew you were a Christian. Of course! I've always known that. But here's the thing about Christianity. I expect more, not less, compassion from Christians than from non-believers.

If you're using Christianity to justify the post you made, I think we still need to talk about that.

The story of Sodom and Gomorrah, which modern Christianity uses to justify hate toward my community, is not about sodomy. No, it's about inhospitality. Read Mel White's Stranger at the Gate. He read the story in the original Hebrew and explains it in that book.

Also, we don't choose to be gay, but we do choose not to live a lie. Society is hard enough on us, even without Christianity. I would love to see Christians, especially Evangelicals, embrace compassion more.

Yours,

- Susan

* * *

Dear Susan,

I saw your mother at the pharmacy yesterday. She sure is looking her age. Do you take after her much?

- Bonnie

***

Susan,

I'm so excited, I had to write you again right away. We are going on a cruise! We'll fly to Miami first, then spend 2 weeks hopping from sunny port to sunny port. Cancun and Cozumel, here we come! I can't wait to have fruity drinks on the beach, seafood right out of the sea. Remember that time we actually got a table at that famous fish place in Boston? I'm already reading menus for our trip. Thought of you.

- Bonnie

***

Hi Susan,

Our church has been sending letters to neighbors across the city to spread the Word in these terrible times. People are afraid to open their doors to us, so we are using letters to minister. We just don't get any exercise by licking stamps!

Anyway, yours is in the mail. I hope it brings you comfort and peace. As I say in the letter, Christianity offers hope of eternal life that will be much better than the life we have here – it'll be perfect, as will we. The Bible is an investment in your future that I hope you will make.

Love,

- Bonnie

* * *

Bonnie.

I have been so busy! I wanted to write sooner but life just keeps getting in the way. Weird, even though I no longer have a commute, I'm still struggling to find time to do things. I only have a sec. I heard about the big Jan 6 anniversary party from Dad. He's considering going. Perhaps you'll see him there?

Stay well,

- Susan

* * *

Hello Susan,

Yes, we're going to the party! It's on Epiphany Day! Should be a lot of fun, especially seeing like-hearted friends we haven't seen in a while. They're going to set up a live video feed so we can watch speeches from the protest in DC. I'll look for your dad. Does he have natural immunity now too?

Did you get the letter?

- Bonnie

***

Dear Bonnie,

I did get your letter. Thank you for your heartfelt concern for my soul in the afterlife you believe in. I do hope to stay here on Earth a while longer, and will rely on man's scientific discoveries and modern medicine to help me do that.

You know, I don't think science and religion have to be enemies. If there is a God and if that God gave humans the ability to reason and to develop scientific knowledge, I would hope you'd respect those gifts from God – and God's belief in us.

Free will allows you to choose both your religion and your politics. Does it have to be us and them? Christian and not? Southern and not? Red State, Blue State? Educated vs. Believers? (BTW, ANTIFA stands for anti-fascist; what is wrong with being ANTI-FASCIST in a supposed-democracy?).

Anyway. It's not my team vs. your team. It's not football. If there is common ground, we the people need to find it.

I hope we can.

- Susan

Background Noise

I should've known I was dying when the background noise stopped.

Chris. S. Witwer lives in Bethesda, Maryland, with her wife, Shi and their two cats, Molly Ivins and Stella Floof.